Dear Parent:

Congratulations! Your child is taking the first steps on an exciting journey. The destination? Independent reading!

STEP INTO READING® will help your child get there. The program offers books at five levels that accompany children from their first attempts at reading to reading success. Each step includes fun stories, fiction and nonfiction, and colorful art. There are also Step into Reading Sticker Books, Step into Reading Math Readers, and Step into Reading Phonics Readers— a complete literacy program with something to interest every child.

Learning to Read, Step by Step!

Ready to Read   Preschool–Kindergarten
• big type and easy words • rhyme and rhythm • picture clues
For children who know the alphabet and are eager to begin reading.

Reading with Help   Preschool–Grade 1
• basic vocabulary • short sentences • simple stories
For children who recognize familiar words and sound out new words with help.

Reading on Your Own   Grades 1–3
• engaging characters • easy-to-follow plots • popular topics
For children who are ready to read on their own.

Reading Paragraphs   Grades 2–3
• challenging vocabulary • short paragraphs • exciting stories
For newly independent readers who read simple sentences with confidence.

Ready for Chapters   Grades 2–4
• chapters • longer paragraphs • full-color art
For children who want to take the plunge into chapter books but still like colorful pictures.

STEP INTO READING® is designed to give every child a successful reading experience. The grade levels are only guides. Children can progress through the steps at their own speed, developing confidence in their reading, no matter what their grade.

Remember, a lifetime love of reading starts with a single step!

For Mallory, my good buddy
—H.K.

www.stepintoreading.com

Educators and librarians, for a variety of teaching tools, visit us at www.randomhouse.com/teachers

Library of Congress Cataloging-in-Publication Data
Kilgras, Heidi.
Me too, Woody! / by Heidi Kilgras ; illustrated by Philippe Harchy.
   p.   cm. — (Step into reading. A step 1 book)   "Toy Story 2."
SUMMARY: Jessie feels left out when Woody and Buzz play checkers and seesaw together, but when they start a baseball game, she and the other toys get to join the game.
ISBN 0-7364-1266-2 (trade) — ISBN 0-7364-8004-8 (lib. bdg.)
[1. Toys—Fiction.]
I. Harchy, Philippe, ill.   II. Title.   III. Series: Step into reading. Step 1 book.
PZ7.K5553   Me   2003   [E]—dc21   2002013343

Printed in the United States of America   11 10 9 8 7 6 5 4 3 2

DISNEY · PIXAR

TOY STORY 2

Me Too, Woody!

by Heidi Kilgras

illustrated by Atelier Philippe Harchy

Random House 🏠 New York

Buzz and Woody.

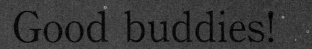
Good buddies!

Game time.

Checkers!

"Me too, Woody!"

Buzz and Woody.

Good buddies!

Playtime.

Seesaw!

"Me too, Woody!"

"No, only two."

Poor Jessie!

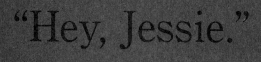

"Hey, Jessie."

"Want to play?"

"Yay!"

Play ball!

Big swing.

Big hit!

"Run, Buzz!"

"Run, Jessie!"

Going.

Going.

Got it!

Good play!
Good buddies!